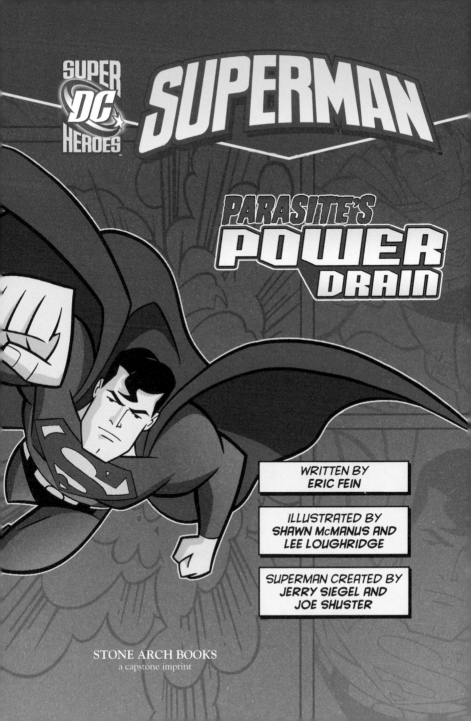

Published by Stone Arch Books in 2010
A Capstone Imprint
151 Good Counsel Drive, P.O. Box 669
Mankato, Minnesota 56002
www.capstonepub.com

Library of Congress Cataloging-in-Publication Data

Fein, Eric.
  Parasite's power drain / by Eric Fein ; illustrated by Shawn McManus ;
illustrated by Lee Loughridge.
      p. cm. -- (DC super heroes. Superman)
  ISBN 978-1-4342-1882-7 (library binding) -- ISBN 978-1-4342-2261-9
(pbk.)
  [1. Superheroes--Fiction.] I. McManus, Shawn, ill. II. Loughridge, Lee, ill.
III. Title.
  PZ7.F3337Par 2010
  [Fic]--dc22   2009029101

Summary: As the sun sets in Metropolis, the electricity suddenly goes
out, and a crime wave erupts throughout the darkened city. This is a job
for Superman! But as the Man of Steel restores order, an even bigger
problem arrives . . . the evil Parasite. This power-hungry monster won't let
Superman save the day without a fight. If the Man of Steel isn't careful,
it'll be lights out for him as well.

Art Director: Bob Lentz
Designer: Hilary Wacholz
Production Specialist: Michelle Biedscheid

Printed in the United States of America in Stevens Point, Wisconsin.
092009
005619WZS10

TABLE OF CONTENTS

CHAPTER 1

DON'T MESS WITH LEX

Lex Luthor stood before the Metropolis City Council and smiled. He cut a striking figure with his bald head and hand-tailored suit. He looked at the council members. He disliked every single one of them.

"In closing," he said, "LexCorp's Power Grid System, the L-9000, will protect Metropolis from citywide blackouts. I know the price for it seems high. Don't worry, it will end up paying for itself over time."

"That's easy for you to say, Mr. Luthor," Councilman Robert Peters said.

"I think more study of your system is needed," Robert Peters continued. "It is clear that the L-9000 could be valuable to the city. However, I am not comfortable with the price you're asking."

Whispers of agreement rippled through the council chamber. Luthor's response was to smile. His face gave no hint of the anger that was boiling up inside of him. *How dare Councilman Peters question me!* he thought.

"Fine," Luthor said. "Study the plan to your heart's content. You'll learn soon enough that your city needs the L-9000."

He snapped his fingers. His assistant and bodyguard, Mercy Graves, marched over. She had been standing to the side.

The meeting had been open to the general public and the news media.

Now, they were all shouting questions at Luthor. He did not respond. The *Daily Planet* newspaper had sent reporter Lois Lane and photographer Jimmy Olsen. They both stood near the exit. **CLICK! CLICK!** Jimmy was snapping dozens of photos of the scene.

"Wow, that was some meeting, wasn't it, Ms. Lane?" Jimmy said. **CLICK!**

"Yes," Lois said. "It's nice to see old Lex put in his place once in a while. Here he comes now."

Mercy Grave was in front of Lex Luthor, pushing people out of the way. Lois managed to step out in front of him. She held her mini-recorder up to his face.

"Any comments on being turned down, Lex?" she said.

"The city council has Metropolis's best interests at heart," he said. "And I'm sure that they will come to see things my way. Good day, Ms. Lane."

Outside, Luthor's limousine was waiting. Mercy opened the rear passenger door and held it for Luthor.

"Peters thinks he has the upper hand," Luthor said as he got in. "I'll show him. I'll show Metropolis that there is a high price to pay for going against me."

Later, Lex Luthor stood in his office atop the LexCorp building. He gazed out of the tall windows. Night was falling on Metropolis. The city's sleek buildings gleamed in the moonlight.

"You wanted to see me, Luthor?" It was a man's voice, gruff and cold.

Luthor turned to face the man standing in the middle of his office. The man wore a wide-brimmed hat pulled down over his face, and a long, brown trench coat.

"Have a seat," Luthor said.

"I'll stand," the man said. "So what do you need from me?"

"I don't need anything from you," Luthor said. "I brought you here because I have a plan that will benefit both of us."

"I'm listening," the man said.

"Metropolis has to be reminded that it needs me," Luthor said. "I'm the one who creates the projects that bring money and jobs into this city."

"Yeah, yeah," the man said. "I get the point. You're a regular man of the people."

"There is nothing regular about me," Luthor responded. "I want you to take Metropolis offline. Drive it into darkness, and bring the city to a standstill. And I want you to make it look like a flaw in the power company's system."

"That's no simple task you want done," the man said. "It's sure to get Superman's attention."

"Are you afraid of that overgrown do-gooder?" Luthor asked.

"Parasite ain't afraid of Superman!" the man said. **THUD!** He slammed his purple fists on Lex's desk as he stepped forward. Mercy moved from her post, but Lex gestured for her to stay there.

"Taking down Superman is going to cost you big time, Luthor," Parasite said.

Parasite sat back down. "It'll cost you ten million dollars in cash," he said.

"You'll do it for five million, Rudy. Count yourself lucky that I chose you for the job," Luthor said. "Who do you think arranged your escape from prison on Stryker's Island? Of course, if five million isn't enough, I can have you sent back to jail today. The choice is up to you."

"I'll do it," Parasite said. "Just have my money ready for me."

"Of course," Luthor said. "Go to the Swan Hotel. There is a room reserved for you. You will be contacted in a few days with your instructions."

"Sure thing, boss," Parasite said.

After Parasite was gone, Luthor called Mercy over.

"Yes, Mr. Luthor?" she asked.

"I want you to keep a close eye on our purple friend," he said. "Make sure he behaves himself until the job is done."

"Yes, Mr. Luthor," she said.

CHAPTER 2

LIGHTS OUT!

The Metropolis Power Company sat at the edge of town. The company's giant generators ran twenty-four hours a day, seven days a week. It was protected by armed guards and an electric fence. None of that worried Parasite.

It had been a week since Parasite had met with Lex Luthor. Now, he stood at the power plant. He was waiting for one person, Henry Hertz. Hertz was the chief engineer of the plant. Parasite had been waiting there an hour when Hertz arrived.

When he saw Hertz walk by, Parasite reached out and grabbed him. ZZZRRRRRTT! Parasite could feel himself absorb Hertz's bioenergy and memories. The purple thug now knew the layout of the plant and how to shut down the generators.

When he was finished absorbing, Parasite threw the unconscious man into the bushes. Then he leaped into the air over the electric fence. He landed out of range of the security cameras. *So far so good,* he thought. Now, he had to get inside unseen.

"Hey, who are you?" a man asked.

Parasite turned to find an armed security guard moving toward him.

So much for Luthor's careful planning, Parasite thought.

POP! The guard was able to get off one shot to raise an alarm before Parasite grabbed him. The villain absorbed all of the guard's bioenergy and then left him knocked out on the ground. Parasite ran to a locked side entrance and kicked it open. This set off more alarms.

BEEP! BEEP! The alarm rang in the plant's security control room. Two security officers, Bob and Ray, were watching the video monitors. They were terrified by what they saw. Parasite was tossing aside guards like paper dolls.

"He's heading for the generator room!" Bob yelled.

"If he destroys the generators," Ray added, "Metropolis will come to a stop!"

Bob dialed police headquarters.

"This is Bob Reynolds at the Metropolis Power Company," he said into the phone. "We're under attack from Parasite!"

"We need more than the police," Ray said. "We need Superman!"

At that very moment, Superman was across town. He was disguised as Clark Kent, reporter for the *Daily Planet* newspaper. Clark was hard at work on an article for the *Planet's* morning edition. He was writing an article about Metropolis's energy problems.

Nearby, Lois Lane was at her desk. She was writing another article about Lex Luthor and the Metropolis City Council.

Jimmy Olsen sat in a chair next to Clark's desk. He was putting a new memory card into his camera.

"Hey, Smallville," Lois said, using her nickname for Clark. "How's that article coming? You need any help?"

Clark didn't mind the nickname. He was proud of being raised in Smallville, Kansas.

"Thanks, Lois, but I'm nearly finished," he said.

"Kent! Lane! Get in here," yelled their boss, Perry White.

Both reporters rushed over to White's office. Though he was not called, Jimmy tagged along. He slipped in just as White was closing the door. Jimmy gave him a sheepish smile.

Perry White grunted and sat at his desk. "I want both of you to get down to the Metropolis Power Company. I just got a tip that it's under attack," he said.

"Golly!" Jimmy said. "I'm glad I just recharged my camera's flash. I'm ready to go, Chief."

"Olsen!" White yelled. "How many times have I told you not to call me Chief!"

"Too many times," Jimmy mumbled, head bowed. "Sorry."

Clark knew he had to find an excuse to slip away and turn into Superman.

"Uh, Mr. White," Clark said, "maybe Lois should head on down there first. I can go over to city hall and get some background details."

"Nothing doing," Perry snapped. "I want you both down there . . . now."

"Yeah, Clark," Lois said. "What's the deal? You running away from what could be the biggest story of the year?"

"Do you know something we don't?" she added.

"No," Clark said.

"Well, then let's go!" Jimmy shouted. FLASH! As they headed for the elevator, the lights suddenly went out.

"Uh-oh," Jimmy said.

In the dark, they turned to look out the window. What they saw chilled them. Metropolis was in the middle of a blackout.

"Come on," Lois said. "I've got a flashlight in my desk. We'll take the stairs."

"Okay, Ms. Lane," Jimmy said.

"We're in for some night, huh, Clark?" Lois said. "Clark? Are you there?"

There was no reply.

"Now where did he go?" she said.

Clark had used the darkness to slip away. Now, he used his super-vision to guide him through the dark. He ducked into a little-used storage closet.

Seconds later, a red and blue blur flew from the Daily Planet and into the sky.

CHAPTER 3

TRAPPED!

The police had the power company surrounded by the time Superman showed up. He would have arrived sooner, but he had to rescue people trapped in elevators all over Metropolis. Thanks to super-speed, he was able to save them all in minutes.

Superman landed in front of the police officer in command, Lt. Maggie Sawyer. She was in charge of the Metropolis Special Crimes Unit. He had worked with her before and liked her. She was a very smart and friendly police officer.

"What's the situation, Maggie?" asked the Man of Steel.

"Parasite," she said. "He broke in and shut down the generators. We have no idea why."

"Did the power company workers manage to escape?" Superman asked.

"We believe everyone got out. But we're doing a head count to make sure," Maggie answered.

"Good," he said. "Then I'm going in."

"You could be walking into a trap," she warned.

Superman smiled. "It wouldn't be the first time," he said.

The Man of Steel bravely flew into the darkened power company.

As he did, Lois and Jimmy arrived. Lois parked her car behind the crowd and got out. She ran into a nearby group of trees, a nervous Jimmy following. Then she took off again.

Now, Lois hid behind a deserted truck. Jimmy was right next to her.

"Ms. Lane, are you crazy?" Jimmy asked. "You can get in big trouble for this."

"A good reporter doesn't let anything stop her from getting the story," Lois said. "Besides, this is bigger than just some scoop. Are you with me?"

Jimmy gulped hard. "I must be nuts," he said. "Yeah, I'm with you."

"That's the spirit," Lois said. "Hang on to your camera and follow me." Lois darted into the company's parking lot.

She used the parked cars for cover. Jimmy did his best to keep up with her. At a side entrance there were only two police officers on guard. Lois picked up a pebble and threw it over the officers' heads. **CLINK** The pebble landed several feet away. It made just enough noise to attract the officers' attention. They walked over to see what had caused the sound.

"Now's our chance, Jimmy," she said. "Let's go!"

Lois yanked open the door. They quickly ran inside before the police returned.

Meanwhile, Superman used his X-ray vision to search for Parasite. The villain was nowhere to be seen. Superman wondered if Parasite had already escaped, but he had to be sure. If he needed to, he would search every inch of the building.

Superman made his way to the power room. It was as big as an airplane hangar. Parasite had tipped over one of the generators.

Again, Superman used his X-ray vision to search the room. There was still no sign of Parasite. Then he heard a crackling sound and looked up. It was Parasite. He had been hiding on the support beams of the ceiling. Parasite jumped at Superman.

"Don't mind me," Parasite said. "I just dropped in for a snack — you!"

He punched Superman in the jaw. The contact between their skins had a sudden effect on both of them. Parasite absorbed Superman's powers and memories. He instantly became as strong as the Man of Steel, and he knew Superman's secret. *Superman is Clark Kent!* realized Parasite.

The blow had also weakened Superman. Parasite struck him again, growing more powerful by the second. Superman continued to become weaker with each hit.

KRASCHHH!! Superman smashed into one of the generators. Parasite flew down and landed next to him. He picked up the knocked-out hero and held him above his head.

"Put him down, you bully!" Lois yelled.

Parasite snapped his head in Lois and Jimmy's direction. He sorted through Superman's memories to learn who the two strangers were. Lois Lane, a reporter. Superman has feelings for her. Jimmy Olsen was Superman's pal. The Man of Steel cared about these people a great deal.

Parasite smiled at Lois.

"Your wish is my command!" Parasite bellowed, throwing Superman at them.

KA-BOOM! Superman crash-landed where they had been standing. They barely managed to get out of the way. The impact sent Superman straight through the floor and into the basement, leaving a large hole.

"Superman!" Lois shouted into the hole. "Are you okay?"

Suddenly, a shadow fell over her and Jimmy. They looked up. Parasite was floating above them.

"If I were you, I'd stop worrying about him and start worrying about yourself," said Parasite.

CHAPTER 4

TO THE RESCUE

Superman opened his eyes. He was in the basement of the power company. He was pinned to the floor under a ton of concrete and steel beams. Parasite's attack had left him weak and in pain.

Superman could hear Lois and Jimmy struggling with Parasite. He heard Parasite say to Jimmy, "You bother me, kid." **KRAK!** Then came the sound of Jimmy hitting the floor.

Superman took hold of the largest piece of concrete that lay across his chest.

He took a deep breath and pushed with all his might. The concrete and beams groaned as they gave way under his strength. His muscles trembled from effort.

There were a few seconds where he didn't think that he'd be able to do it. However, he refused to give up and disregarded the burning pain in his muscles. Finally, the concrete and beams let loose. *RUMMMMMMMBLE!* He flew up and floated into the room. He spotted Jimmy Olsen lying in a corner.

"Jimmy," he said. "Are you okay?"

Jimmy sat up and rubbed his head.

"Yeah," Jimmy said. "Just a bad headache."

"Sit tight," Superman said. "I'll have you out of here in a minute."

Superman went to work. He moved the generator back into its regular position and repaired whatever he could.

He noticed a worker's protective suit lying in a knocked-over storage locker. He took the gloves from the suit and tucked them into his belt.

Then he flew to Jimmy and lifted him.

"Okay, Jimmy," he said. "Let's go."

He flew them high above the building. He searched the area for any sign of Lois. She was nowhere to be seen. Superman used his super-hearing to locate her. He heard Lois say to Parasite, "Why did you take me to the Daily Planet building?"

"It means something to Superman," Parasite said. "I want to see the pain on his face when I destroy it — and you."

Superman left Jimmy with Maggie Sawyer so he could get medical attention. He explained how he put the generator back into place. The power company would now be able to start it up again. Then, he took off for the Daily Planet. As he did, he spotted Mercy Graves in the crowd. *Lex Luthor must have a hand in tonight's events,* thought Superman. *But I don't have time to question his bodyguard. I have to save Lois.*

On top of the roof of the Daily Planet building spun a giant globe. The Planet's sign was wrapped around it. Parasite had tied Lois to the sign.

"You're in big trouble, Parasite," Lois said. "Superman will send you back to jail."

Parasite laughed. "In a few minutes, Ms. Lane, you and your superpowered friend will be dead!"

"That's what you think," Superman said.

Parasite and Lois looked up to see the Man of Steel speeding toward them. His arms were stretched out in front of him. On his hands he wore the gloves he had removed from the protective suit.

Parasite didn't move fast enough. He felt the full force of Superman's fist hitting him right in the chest. **WHAM!** The blow sent him crashing into a nearby high-rise building. He roared with anger and flew back at Superman, but missed him.

"I can do this all day," Superman said. "What about you?"

"How about a game of catch?" Parasite said. Parasite landed on the roof of the Daily Planet. He lifted the giant globe up out of its base. **RUMMMMMMMBLE!**

Terror washed over Superman. Lois was still tied to the globe. "Stop!" Superman shouted. "Leave Lois alone! She's done nothing to you."

"Yes, but if you are busy rescuing her, then you can't catch me," Parasite said.

WHOOOOSH! He threw the globe as if it were a giant baseball. Lois screamed as she spun through the air.

Superman threw the gloves to the ground and closed the distance between himself and the falling globe. Then, he was in front of it. He landed in the middle of the street, the globe speeding at him. Superman held open his arms. He caught the globe and set it down safely on the street. He freed Lois and grabbed the gloves. The Man of Steel didn't wait for her thanks. He had to catch Parasite.

CHAPTER 5

THE BATTLE FOR METROPOLIS

Parasite turned to see a very angry Man of Steel flying right at him.

From his penthouse office, Lex Luthor watched the fight. His building had its own private source of electricity, so it was not affected by the blackout. His cell phone rang, and it was Mercy.

"Mr. Luthor, your plan is falling apart!" she said.

"Yes," Luthor said. "I've noticed. Return to the office."

Oh well, he thought. *At least I've managed to make two of my enemies fight each other. That's worth something.*

Outside, Parasite and Superman battled in midair. The gloves Superman wore let him hold onto Parasite without losing any of his powers. Parasite struggled to free himself from the hero's grip. He brushed the top of his head against the bottom of Superman's jaw, giving himself a boost of power and weakening Superman.

Parasite twisted free and grabbed Superman's cape. Then, Parasite threw his enemy like a rag doll. **CRASH!** His body flew into an office building and out the other side.

Parasite laughed and flew after the Man of Steel, who had crashed in the middle of the street.

A Metropolis city bus screeched to a stop in front of the fallen hero. Parasite flew down and picked the bus up. He flew with it into the sky, and he waited until Superman was back on his feet.

"Flying too hard on you? Then try the bus!" Parasite said. He threw the huge vehicle at Superman.

"No!" Superman shouted, as he rushed to catch it. The passengers screamed.

"Don't panic," Superman said. "I've got you!"

He set the bus down. But as he did, Parasite smashed into him, sending him crashing across the street. CRUNCH!

Superman landed by a fire hydrant. He looked up to see Parasite flying toward him.

Suddenly, the lights came on all over Metropolis. The power company's engineers had been able to restart the generators.

"Stay put," Parasite said. "I'm running low on energy. I need more of your power."

Superman waited until Parasite was very close, and then he sprang into action. His arm struck the hydrant. **SPLASH!** A powerful stream of water shot out, hitting Parasite. The blast sent him flying across the street. Superman used his super-speed to beat Parasite to the other side.

CHING! He pulled a street lamp out of its base, and held it like a giant baseball bat. At just the right moment, Superman swung the lamp, slamming it into Parasite. **KA-POW!** He bounced off of it and flew high in the sky. Parasite crashed into a giant neon sign. **BZZT!**

BOOM! The contact with the soaking wet Parasite caused an electrical explosion.

Parasite screamed and then passed out. Superman flew to his side to take his pulse. He was breathing, but unconscious. Superman twisted the lamppost around Parasite to restrain him.

When he came to, Parasite was confused. "What happened?" he said. "Where am I?"

The shock had caused Parasite to lose his memory. Superman was relieved. Parasite had forgotten all the memories he had drained from Superman. Clark's secret identity was safe!

Superman handed Parasite over to the police. Then he took off for his final stop of the night.

"I'd like a word with you, Lex," Superman said. He was floating outside Luthor's penthouse office window.

Luthor sighed. "What now?"

"I know you're the one behind the blackout," Superman said.

"I don't know what you are talking about," Luthor replied.

"I spotted Mercy at the power plant. Did you have her drive Parasite there?" Superman asked.

"If she was there, I'm sure it was as a concerned citizen," Luthor said with a smile. "Now, you'll have to excuse me. I need to get back to work on my new proposal for the L-9000. The price for the city to purchase it just doubled."

Now, it was Superman's turn to smile.

"That won't be necessary, Lex," Superman said. "I met with Professor Emil Hamilton at S.T.A.R. Labs since you first announced your L-9000. He's working on a power grid system similar to yours. However, his version is a lot cheaper."

The veins in Luthor's temples and forehead pounded. His mouth became a thin line. In a low but angry tone he said, "Nicely played, Superman."

With that, the Man of Steel flew off into the night.

Luthor stood outside his empty office. "You won this battle Superman," he said. "But the war is far from over."

DAILY PLANET

WHO IS PARASITE?

As Rudy Jones's gambling addiction grew, so did his debts. To pay them off, he attempted to steal experimental chemicals from a laboratory in Metropolis. When Superman intervened, Rudy fled. During his escape, he accidentally exposed himself to toxic liquids, transforming him into the power-hungry monster Parasite. Forever changed, Rudy developed a new addiction: the desire for power. Parasite must regularly feed on the energy of others, or he will wither and die.

- Parasite poses a unique problem to anyone who stands in his way: his energy-sucking, parasitic powers let him rise to the level of any foe simply by touching them. The more powerful his opponent is, the more threatening Parasite becomes.

- Parasite possesses the ability to steal the thoughts of his victims as well as their powers. If Parasite ever drained enough of Superman's strength, he would discover the Man of Steel's true identity!

- Having grown bored with draining human energy, Parasite went after Mr. Mxyzptlk, the mischievous, magical imp from the Fifth Dimension. After stealing Mxy's strange powers, he spread chaos across Metropolis, turning Lois Lane and Jimmy Olsen into super-villains. He even made a Superman statue come to life!

- Once Parasite tasted Superman's massive power, he knew no other energy would ever satisfy him. Parasite will do whatever it takes to once again get within reach of the Man of Steel, or his superpowered cousin, Supergirl.

BIOGRAPHIES

Eric Fein is a freelance writer and editor. He has edited books for Marvel and DC Comics, which included well-known characters such as Batman, Superman, Wonder Woman, and Spider-Man. Fein has also written dozens of graphic novels and educational children's books. He currently lives in Ridgefield Park, New Jersey.

Shawn McManus has been drawing pictures ever since he was able to hold a pencil in his tiny little hand. Since then, he has illustrated comic books featuring Sandman, Batman, Dr. Fate, Spider-Man, and many others. Shawn has also done work for film, animation, and online entertainment. He lives in New England, and he loves the spring season there.

Lee Loughridge has been working in comics for more than 14 years. He currently lives in sunny California in a tent on the beach.

GLOSSARY

generator (JEN-uh-ray-tur)—a machine that produces electricity by turning a magnet inside a coil of wire

gestured (JESS-churd)—moved your hands or head in order to communicate a feeling or idea

relieved (ri-LEEVD)—eased trouble or pain

restrain (ri-STRAYN)—prevent someone from doing something, or hold something back

sheepish (SHEEP-ish)—if someone looks sheepish, the person looks embarrassed or ashamed for doing something silly or foolish

standstill (STAND-still)—if something is at a standstill, it has come to a complete halt

terrified (TER-uh-fyed)—frightened greatly, or filled with terror

villain (VIL-uhn)—an evil person

DISCUSSION QUESTIONS

1. Superman knew Luthor was guilty, but he couldn't prove it. Should Superman have arrested him anyway? Why or why not?

2. Lois and Jimmy sneak into the power plant without permission to get the story for the *Daily Planet*. Is it ever okay to deceive or trick someone? Explain.

3. Who is more to blame in this book — Lex Luthor or Parasite? Why?

WRITING PROMPTS

1. Parasite has been captured, and *you* have to think of a way to keep him in prison! How would you design his jail cell? What safety measures would you use to protect others? Write about it.

2. What are some other ways Superman could've defeated Parasite without touching him? Write about another way Superman stops Parasite.

3. Think up your own super-villain. What powers does he have? What weaknesses? Write about your villain, and then draw a picture of him.

MORE NEW
SUPERMAN
ADVENTURES!

DEEP SPACE HIJACK

LITTLE GREEN MEN

LIVEWIRE!

THE DEADLY DOUBLE

THE KID WHO SAVED SUPERMAN